Domino
Jess
Tommy
Seal
peggy
Max
Ekky

First published in Great Britain in 2001 by David & Charles Children's Books, a division of David & Charles Limited
First published in the United States by Holiday House, Inc., in 2001
 Printed in Belgium. First Edition. www.holidayhouse.com

Library of Congress Cataloging-in-Publication Data
Cabrera, Jane.
Old Mother Hubbard / Jane Cabrera.–1st ed.
p. cm.
Based on The comic adventures of Old Mother Hubbard and her dog, by Sarah Catherine Martin,
originally published in London, 1805, by John Harris.
Summary: Light-hearted illustrations accompany this version of the familiar nursery rhyme
about an old woman and her playful dog.
ISBN 0-8234-1659-3 (hardcover)
1. Dogs–Juvenile poetry. 2. Nursery rhymes. 3. Children's poetry, English.
[1. Nursery rhymes. 2. English poetry. 3. Dogs–Poetry.]
I. Martin, Sarah Catherine, 1768–1826. Old Mother Hubbard. II. Title.
PZ8.3.C122 O1 2001
821'.7–dc21 00-059715

HOLIDAY HOUSE / New York

Old Mother Hubbard went to the cupboard

to fetch
her poor
dog
a bone.

But when
she got there,
the cupboard
was bare,
and so the
poor dog
had none.

She went to the tailor's

to buy him a coat.

SHOW
Joseph's DREAMCOATS
40
Jack Horner Chairs
42

But when she came back, he was riding a goat.

She went to
the hatter's

to buy him
a hat.

But when she
came back,
he was washing
the cat.

She went to the barber's

to buy him a wig.

But when she came back,
he was dancing a jig.

She went to
the cobbler's

to buy him
some shoes.

But when
she came back,
he was reading
the news.

DAILY DOG
little dog laughs to see such FUN!
One man and dog mow meadow in crop protest.

Then the
dame made
a curtsy,

the dog
made a bow.

The dame said,
"Your Supper!"
The dog
said...

"Bow-Wow!"

Bob
Oz
Brit
Fog
Tess
Higgins
Bob
Lupin